MW01231712

10 Things You Need to Know About

Bullies

by Jen Jones

Consultant:
Allan L. Beane, PhD
Bully Free Systems LLC
www.bullyfree.com

Capstone
press

Mankato, Minnesota

Snap Books are published by Capstone Press,
151 Good Counsel Drive, P.O. Box 669, Mankato, Minnesota 56002.
www.capstonepress.com

Copyright © 2008 by Capstone Press, a Capstone Publishers company.
All rights reserved. No part of this publication may be reproduced in whole or
in part, or stored in a retrieval system, or transmitted in any form or by any means, electronic,
mechanical, photocopying, recording, or otherwise, without written permission of the publisher.
For information regarding permission, write to Capstone Press,
151 Good Counsel Drive, P.O. Box 669, Dept. R, Mankato, Minnesota 56002.
Printed in the United States of America in North Mankato, Minnesota.

082009
005600R

Library of Congress Cataloging-in-Publication Data
Jones, Jen.
    Bullies / by Jen Jones.
    p. cm. — (Snap books. 10 things you need to know about)
    Includes bibliographical references and index.
    Summary: "Provides helpful information and strategies for dealing with
bullies at school and in social settings" — Provided by publisher.
    ISBN-13: 978-1-4296-1343-9 (hardcover)
    ISBN-10: 1-4296-1343-2 (hardcover)
    1. Bullying — Juvenile literature. 2. Bullying in schools — Juvenile
literature. I. Title. II. Series.
BF637.B85J66 2008
302.3'4 — dc22
                                                                        2007028283

Editors: Kathryn Clay and Christine Peterson
Designer: Juliette Peters
Photo Researcher: Jo Miller
Photo Stylist: Kelly Garvin

Photo Credits:
Art Directors/Helene Rogers, 17 (bottom right); Art Directors/Spencer Grant, 12–13; Capstone Press/Karon Dubke, cover,
5, 7, 8–9, 14–15 (all), 16–17 (middle), 18, 19, 20, 21, 22, 24–25, 26, 27; Getty Images Inc./Photonica/Nancy Honey, 11;
Getty Images Inc./Stone/Erik Dreyer, 23; Michele Torma Lee, 32

Table of Contents

Introduction

Ever wonder why kids bully others? It's hard to understand why bullies do what they do. If you've been bullied, remember that it's not your fault. No one deserves to suffer physical or emotional abuse. With this book, you'll start to understand why bullying happens. You'll also get some ideas on how to deal with it.

Over time, bullying can cause serious problems for victims. Their schoolwork may suffer. Fun activities may become worry-filled. Bullying can even damage self-esteem and cause depression.

Bullying can be stopped. This book will show you how to rise above bullying and make your school a safer place. Whether you're a victim, a bystander, or even a bully, prepare to walk away empowered and inspired. Get ready to change the world — one bully at a time!

1 If you're being bullied, you're not alone

Half of all kids are bullied at some point. Bullies are found on playgrounds and buses and in cafeterias and bathrooms. They often choose places where adults aren't likely to be found. Though bullying may be a fact of life, that doesn't make it okay. Bullying behavior is never acceptable.

If you're one of many kids who are bullied regularly, take heart. While it's natural to feel lonely, sad, or afraid, you don't have to feel that way forever. One smart way to deal with bullying is to rally your troops. Talk to your friends, family, and teachers about what's going on. You can also create a support system at school. Spending time with friends or in groups can keep bullies away. The power of friendship can work wonders.

2 Boys and girls bully differently

When it comes to bullying behavior, boys and girls couldn't be more different. Boys tend to fight with their bodies, and girls fight with their minds. While boys might push or hit others, girls are more likely to spread gossip or form cliques.

Boy and girl bullies also choose their victims differently. No one is off-limits for boy bullies. They tend to target both guys and girls. When girls bully, they usually choose other girls as their victims. The main reason for this is their size. Bullies rarely pick on people who are bigger or stronger than they are.

A different meaning

Years ago, being called a bully would have been a compliment. The word comes from the Dutch word boel, which means "loving brother" or "friend."

In the early 1900s, President Theodore Roosevelt also used the word "bully" to express joy. Only more recently did the word take on the negative meaning we know today.

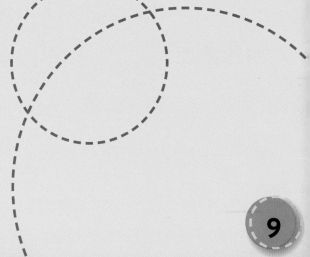

3 Bullying comes in many forms

Bullying behavior can take on many forms. Bullies hurt their victims with words and actions. Experts believe that there are four main kinds of bullying:

❀ Physical bullying involves causing bodily harm to someone else. Hitting, shoving, or other physical attacks are all forms of bullying.

❀ Verbal bullying happens when bullies humiliate their victims with words. If you've ever made fun of others, you've been guilty of verbal bullying.

❀ Cyberbullying involves using technology like the Internet to spread false stories, hurtful messages, or embarrassing pictures of someone else.

❀ Relationship bullying is hard to see but is just as hurtful. This bullying behavior includes leaving someone out of a group or turning friends against someone.

4 Bullying creates a feeling of power

Close your eyes and picture a bully. Did you picture someone big and strong? While that might be the common image, the truth is that bullies come in all shapes and sizes. Bullies can be star athletes or teachers' pets. They can be popular girls or the kids who always get in trouble. What's the one thing they have in common? Hurting others makes bullies feel powerful.

Kids bully for different reasons. In many cases, bullies have learned the behavior from their friends or siblings. They might even be copying something from TV, movies, or video games.

Other times, bullies are abused at home. Being mistreated at home often makes kids feel powerless. Sometimes kids pick on others as a way to regain control in their lives.

Bullies tend to pick on kids who are easily overpowered. Victims often don't hang out with lots of friends. With less people to stick up for the victims, bullies can keep their power.

5 Your reaction can make a difference

When being bullied, it's common to feel alone and afraid. Some victims feel there's nothing they can do to stop bullies. The good news is that there are ways to stop bullies in their tracks. Here are some tips to help you take back your power:

✽ Use the buddy system. Hanging out with friends makes it harder for a bully to single you out.

✽ Stand up for yourself. Telling bullies to stop may catch them by surprise.

✽ Don't fight back physically. Showing your anger gives bullies what they want. Not only will it lead to more bullying, but it could also put you in danger.

✽ Most importantly, tell your parents or teachers — even if a bully has warned you not to. The sooner you tell an adult, the sooner bullies will have to face their actions.

Body Talk

Confident body language is a great way to throw off a bully. Even if you're shaking on the inside, try not to show it. Walk with purpose, make eye contact, and hold your head high. If bullies think you're not scared of them, you won't be an easy target.

6 The bullying tides can turn quickly

In the clique world, a girl might be safe one day, bullied the next. Many girls in cliques are all about being popular. Cliques leave out others so girls in the group feel more powerful. Often one girl steps up as the leader of the group. The leader, or "queen bee," gets to make the rules. The other members feel pressured to do and say the right things. Make one wrong move, and you could be kicked out of the queen bee's clique.

To survive clique behavior, stay true to yourself. The quickest way to weed out fake friends is to dress and act according to your own values. While it might be easy to follow the group, being yourself is always the best choice.

Blume Talks Bullies

Famed kids' book author Judy Blume tackled the subject of bullying in *Blubber*. The 1974 book is still a big hit today because of its true-to-life take on clique politics. The main character, Jill, learns a lot about life and friends. She goes from being part of the popular clique to being their victim.

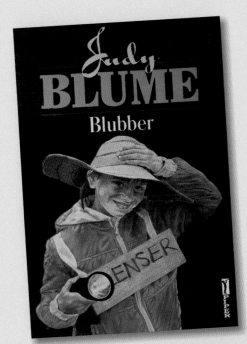

7 Bullying can happen in cyberspace

Cell phones, e-mail, and instant messages can be a girl's best friends. Yet in the hands of a cyberbully, they can also be weapons. Cyberbullies use technology to embarrass or scare their victims. Examples of this kind of bullying include:

❀ Posting embarrassing pictures or mean comments online.

❀ Spreading rumors or sending threatening text or instant messages.

❀ Stealing the victim's password to make a fake profile or send e-mails.

Cyberbullies are often unknown. Many times victims don't find out about the messages until the damage is done. But you shouldn't feel helpless. Tell an adult about hurtful IMs, pictures, or e-mails. Keep passwords to yourself. Finally, don't include anything in an e-mail or text message that you wouldn't want others to read.

8 Students are taking a stand against bullying

Whoever said there is strength in numbers sure knew their stuff. To erase bullying from schools, a group effort must be made by students, parents, and teachers. Many schools have adopted anti-bullying campaigns. Here are some creative ideas to begin one at your school:

❀ Start a "No Blame" peer support group. With a teacher present, students involved in a bullying case gather to talk about it. Without blaming anyone, the teacher helps the kids find a solution.

❀ Create an anti-bullying pledge for students.

❀ Hold a Bullying Awareness Week at school. Events could include discussions, role-playing skits, and talks on bullying.

❀ Set up a secure "Bully Box" for students to write down their experiences in secret. This lets both victims and witnesses report any problems to school officials without fear.

9 Escape the stress caused by bullies

Ever wish you had a secret escape hatch? You're not alone. Bullying can be enough to make anyone want to disappear. Luckily, there are lots of ways to chill out and regroup without having to hide.

One way to calm frazzled nerves is to stay active. Exercise like biking, swimming, or jogging can help build confidence. Another idea is to keep a journal. Writing down your feelings can help you sort through bullying behavior and feel better about yourself. Finally, don't forget the power of friends and family. Talk out your worries. Spend a carefree afternoon with friends at the movies to relieve stress.

10 You don't have to be a bystander

Even if you haven't been bullied, odds are you've seen it happen. About 88 percent of kids say they've witnessed bullying. Maybe you tried to ignore it, or you were angry but didn't know how to help. Perhaps you worried that if you said something, the bully would turn on you.

The truth is that witnesses play an important role in stopping bullies. When someone steps in, the bullying often stops within seconds. So how can you help?

Speak up the next time you see bullying. Bullies may listen when a bystander tells them to stop. Invite the victim to join you and your friends. If you are afraid to step in, find an adult who can help. Afterward, offer support and a caring ear to the victim. Your courage can make a world of difference.

B-I-G Ideas to Stop Bullying

Ready to take action? Use these "B-I-G" ideas to put an end to bullying at your school.

❀ Be aware of your own and your friends' behaviors. Think twice before you make fun of someone's outfit or believe a rumor. Don't let your friends become bullies. If your friends are in the wrong, point out their unkind behavior to them.

❀ Include someone who is being left out. Invite someone to sit with you on the bus or hang out at school.

❀ Go the extra mile and set a good example for others. Treat your classmates how you would like to be treated. Other classmates will soon follow your lead.

25

A Few More Things

You Need to Know

Bullying can lead to serious problems

Victims often feel lasting effects of bullying, even as adults. Bullies might forget about their behavior, but most victims never do. Victims often suffer from depression or low self-esteem. Depression can lead to alcohol and drug abuse. Some victims have taken their own lives. But victims can make positive choices. Turn to friends, family, or a counselor. Avoid alcohol, drugs, or violence.

Bullies often lead troubled lives

Bullying often leads to other unhealthy behaviors. Studies show that bullies are more likely to skip school, use drugs, damage property, and steal. Many of these behaviors don't stop once a bully graduates from high school. In fact, bullies are four times more likely than others to commit a crime by age 24.

Recognize your own bullying behavior

Sometimes you may act like a bully without even knowing it. You might send an e-mail teasing a friend about a new outfit or her latest crush. It's just a joke, right? Not to your friend. Teasing, even in fun, is also bullying. Take note of bullying behavior in your own life. Don't tease or make fun of others. Be a positive leader, and others are sure to follow your example.

Some of your favorite celebrities were bullied as kids

Most Hollywood stars seem cool and confident. But some of them didn't always feel that way. Movie star Kate Winslet was teased about her weight as a child. Actress Rosario Dawson was picked on for her body type. *One Tree Hill* star Chad Michael Murray grew up feeling like he didn't fit in. As a child, Murray had his two front teeth knocked out by a bully. One look at these celebs today shows that a lot can change over the years.

Quiz

Are You at Risk of Becoming a Bully?

When you see someone being picked on, how do you feel?
Ⓐ Uncomfortable — you want to help but don't know how.
Ⓑ Relieved — you're glad that it's not you.
Ⓒ Amused — the bully's words are funny.

What do you think is your strongest weapon against bullies?
Ⓐ Your inner strength
Ⓑ Your smarts
Ⓒ Your friends

Have you ever threatened someone else?
Ⓐ Not that I can remember
Ⓑ Only in a joking way
Ⓒ Yes

After you tease someone, how do you feel?
Ⓐ I try not to tease; you never know what someone is sensitive about.
Ⓑ I don't understand why the other person gets upset.
Ⓒ I feel satisfied that I got under someone's skin.

How would you like the kids at school to see you?
Ⓐ Caring
Ⓑ Popular
Ⓒ Tough

What is most important to you after someone has hurt you?
Ⓐ Talking it out
Ⓑ Forming alliances with other friends
Ⓒ Getting revenge

How likely are you to get in a physical fight at school?
Ⓐ Not likely at all
Ⓑ More likely to get in a non-physical fight
Ⓒ Very likely

A classmate gets a new jacket that you've wanted forever. What's your reaction?
Ⓐ Happy — at least someone can have it.
Ⓑ Jealous — your parents won't buy it for you.
Ⓒ Mad — you'd like that jacket for yourself.

When playing sports, what's the best part?
- Ⓐ Becoming better at something
- Ⓑ Hanging out with my teammates
- Ⓒ Winning

When you get mad at someone, how long does it take you to "get over it?"
- Ⓐ It depends, but I try not to be negative.
- Ⓑ I stay mad for days.
- Ⓒ I hold a grudge forever.

In your opinion, what makes someone else an easy target?
- Ⓐ I don't think of people as targets.
- Ⓑ The person is shy and has poor social skills.
- Ⓒ The person looks different from me or thinks differently than I do.

What makes it okay to tease or roughhouse with someone else?
- Ⓐ When the other person also thinks it's fun.
- Ⓑ When it helps gain acceptance from the other kids.
- Ⓒ It's always okay if I feel like doing it.

Do other people's feelings matter to you?
- Ⓐ Yes
- Ⓑ It depends
- Ⓒ Not really

What do you think are the long-term effects of bullying?
- Ⓐ It could cause serious damage to someone's self-esteem.
- Ⓑ I'm sure the victims get over it after the school year ends.
- Ⓒ Who cares?

What do you think about bullying?
- Ⓐ It needs to be stopped.
- Ⓑ It's a fact of life.
- Ⓒ Some people deserve to be picked on.

When scoring your answers, Ⓐ equals 5 points, Ⓑ equals 3 points, and Ⓒ equals 1 point. Total them up and find out whether you're guilty of bully behavior.

1-25 = Whether you know it or not, you share many qualities of a typical bully. Examine your behavior, and think about how it affects others.

26-50 = You tend to turn a blind eye to bullying and worry about what others might think of you. Remember that clique behavior can often be a form of bullying. Don't be afraid to take a stand.

51-75 = You're not afraid to do what's right, and you treat others with kindness. Your behavior sets a positive example for others. Keep up the good deeds!

Glossary

abuse (uh-BYOOSS) — the wrong or harmful treatment of someone

bystander (BYE-stan-dur) — someone who is at a place where something happens to someone else

clique (KLIK) — a group of friends who do not accept others into their group

depression (di-PRESH-uhn) — an emotional disorder that causes people to feel sad and tired

empower (em-POU-ur) — to supply someone with confidence or an ability

humiliate (hyoo-MIL-ee-ate) — to make someone look or feel foolish or embarrassed

self-esteem (SELF-ess-TEEM) — a feeling of pride and respect for oneself

Read More

Cooper, Scott. *Speak Up and Get Along!: Learn The Mighty Might, Thought Chop, And More Tools To Make Friends, Stop Teasing, And Feel Good About Yourself.* Minneapolis: Free Spirit, 2005.

Hibbert, Adam. *Why Do People Bully?* Exploring Tough Issues. Chicago: Raintree, 2005.

Raum, Elizabeth. *Bullying.* Chicago: Heinemann, 2008.

Internet Sites

FactHound offers a safe, fun way to find Internet sites related to this book. All of the sites on FactHound have been researched by our staff.

Here's how:

1. Visit *www.facthound.com*
2. Choose your grade level.
3. Type in this book ID **1429613432** for age-appropriate sites. You may also browse subjects by clicking on letters, or by clicking on pictures and words.
4. Click on the **Fetch It** button.

FactHound will fetch the best sites for you!

About the Author

Jen Jones is a Los Angeles-based writer and author. Her work has appeared in magazines such as *American Cheerleader, Dance Spirit, Ohio Today*, and *Pilates Style*. She has also written for Web sites like *E! Online*, and *PBS Kids*. Jen has written for the *The Jenny Jones Show, The Sharon Osbourne Show*, and *The Larry Elder Show*. She is also a member of the Society of Children's Book Writers and Illustrators. She recently completed books on gymnastics and fashion for young girls.